Hello, Come In

By Ida DeLage

Drawings by John Mardon

GARRARD PUBLISHING COMPANY
CHAMPAIGN, ILLINOIS

Copyright © 1971 by Ida DeLage   All rights reserved. Manufactured in the U.S.A.
Standard Book Number: 8116–6708–1   Library of Congress Catalog Card Number: 71–156079

891759

Hello, Come In

Hello.

Come in.

I am Grandma.

This is my house.

Sit down.

Sit down, my dear.

Have a cookie.
I made some cookies
just for you.
Have one.
Have two.

Good-bye.
Come again.
The next time
I will make a cake.

Hello.

Come in.

I am a witch.
This is my cave.
Sit down.
Sit down, my pretty.

This is my pot.
I made some brew.
Drink my brew.
It will do
something funny
to you.
Hee-hee-hee.

Good-bye.
Come again.
Come on Halloween.
Hee-hee-hee.

Hello.

Come in.

I am a pig.

This is my pig-pen.

Sit down.

Sit down.

Sit down
in the mud.
Roll in the mud.
Come on.
Roll in the mud
with me.
It is fun, fun, fun.

Good-bye.

Come again.

Come when it rains.

Rain makes good mud.

Hello.

Come in.

I am a ghost.
Sit down.
Sit down.

I haunt this house.

I rattle the windows.

I bang the doors.

Whoo-oo-oo. Whoo-oo-oo.

Good-bye.
Come again.
Come when it is
dark, dark, dark.
Whoo-oo-oo. Whoo-oo-oo.

Hello.

Come in.

I am a frog.

This is my log.

Sit down.

Sit down on my log.

Jump with me.
Jump into the water.
It is fun
in the water.
Have fun with me.
Jump, jump, jump.

Good-bye.

Come again.

Come at night.

I will sing for you.

"Gr-ump. Gr-ump."

Hello.

Come in.

I am a bird.
This is my nest.
I have four babies.
My babies
like to eat.

Do you like to eat?
Here is a bug.
It is for you.
My babies eat bugs.
A bug is good.

891759

Good-bye.
Come again.
Come again
and eat a worm
with me.

Hello.

Come in.

I am a pony.
This is my barn.
Sit down.
Sit down.

Do you like to ride?
Climb on my back.
I will give you a ride.
We can go fast.
It is fun to ride
on my back.

Good-bye.
Come again.
Come again
for a pony ride.

Hello.

Come in.

I am a toymaker.

This is my toy shop.

Sit down.

Sit down.

These are my toys.

I made them.

Do you like toys?

Take a toy.

Do you like a ball?

Do you like a doll?

Good-bye.
Come again.
Come again
and play
with the toys.

Hello.

Come in.

Hello, friends.

This is our house.

Come in.

Come to our party.

Sit down.

Sit down.

Have some cake.

Have some ice cream.

A party is fun.
Have fun
at our party.

Good-bye.
Come again.
Come again, friends.
Come again
to our house.